Enid Blyton

THE BIRTHDAY ADVENTURE

illustrated by **Becka Moor**

Famous Five Colour Short Stories

For a complete list of the full-length
Famous Five adventures, turn to
the last page of this book

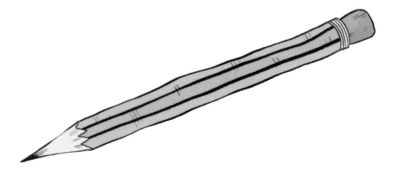

CONTENTS

CHAPTER ONE

'How **lovely** – an invitation to a **party** today!' Anne exclaimed.

'For my friend Alf's birthday!' said George, smiling. **'We're all invited!'**

Anne and her brothers, Julian and Dick,

1

had arrived late the night before to stay with their cousin at Kirrin Cottage for the summer holidays. **The Five were back together again** and George had **hardly** been able to wait until they had sat down for breakfast to show them the invitation.

'I want to get Alf something **really special,**' said George. 'He looked after Timmy for me before Mother and Father allowed him to come and live with us. I don't know what Tim and I would have done without Alf!'

Timmy barked in agreement. **'Woof! Woof!'**

'Well you've left it rather late! How about we all go into Kirrin to buy him something this morning?' said Dick. 'We can choose presents together.'

'Oh blow,' said George. Her face clouded

over as she remembered something. 'I haven't got any pocket money to spend. Father took it away last week because I was making too much *noise* when he was working.'

'**Don't worry,**' said Anne, linking arms with George. 'We've got pocket money. We could all **club together** to buy Alf something.'

George pulled a face. 'I'm not sure that I want to share, though. Alf's one of my **oldest** friends. I'd like to get him something that's **just from me**.'

'Oh for goodness' sake, George!' laughed Julian. 'It's not as though you've got much choice! No pocket money means no present for Alf unless you're willing to go in with us.'

But George couldn't be persuaded, and she started to get **rather sulky.**

'You go into town without me,' she huffed. 'I'm going to take Timmy for a walk instead.'

'Woof!' Timmy barked and jumped up. He was always happy to hear that magic word 'walk'.

George turned on her heels, **slamming** the cottage door behind her.

'What an idiot George can be,' said Dick. **'Maddening.'** Julian shrugged.

'But you know what she's like. Once George has made up her mind about something, there's no changing it.'

CHAPTER TWO

George **stomped** down the path that led to Kirrin Common. Alf was her **friend** and now she couldn't even get him **a birthday present!** Hopefully a walk would cheer her up.

'Come on, Tim,' she called.

The sun was warm, and after they had been walking for a while George began to get quite hot. She turned and headed back towards the beach where there would be a cool breeze.

The beach was normally **quiet** at this
time of morning, but George could already
see a little **motorboat** pulling up to shore.
She frowned. The boat belonged to a local
fisherman but she didn't recognise the two
men in it. They were dressed **all in black** and
looked around carefully before climbing out.

'I wonder what they're **up to,** Timmy,' said George.

All of a sudden, Timmy bounded forward. **'Stop, Tim, stop!'** George called after him.

But it was **too late**.

Timmy was already racing across the sand. Before George could catch her dog, he had reached the men. Now he was tugging at a duffle bag that they were unloading, and **barking loudly.**

He **jumped** around them, getting in their way.

'Control your pesky dog!' one of the men **snarled.**

'You should have that **mutt** on a lead,' the other agreed.

'Timmy doesn't **need** to be on a lead; he's just being friendly,' George snapped.

But the two men had already turned their backs on George and were **marching away** along the shore.

'How rude,' said George.

The sun was now **high** in the **sky.**

George tugged off her shoes and socks, and started to **splash** through the waves. Then she walked along the shore, letting the sand **squelch** through her toes.

'We should head back soon, Tim,' she said finally. **'Oh, but what's that?'**

George had caught sight of something down in the shallows and bent down to pick it up.

17

'It's a **box!**' she exclaimed. 'And a quite lovely one too. Look, Timmy . . .' Each side was decorated with the most **beautiful carvings** of fish and boats. It looked as though it might have once belonged to a **sea captain** and was clearly very old. Perhaps it had been washed up from one of the **shipwrecks,** of which there were plenty in the coves. It had a thick layer of varnish on it, which must have prevented it from rotting in the water.

'What a spot of good luck, Timmy,' said George, **beaming.** 'This will make the **perfect present** for Alf!'

CHAPTER THREE

George and Timmy crossed the sands and
started to weave their way back up the path
to **Kirrin Cottage.** Once, George stopped to
take a stone out of her shoe and she got the
strangest feeling that they were being
followed.

Finally they reached the gate to the little white-stoned house that was home. Roses climbed the walls and flowers filled the front garden.

George walked up the path and in through the front door, dumping her shoes and socks in the hallway.

'At last! **There** you are,' Aunt Fanny, George's mother, called out. 'We wondered where you had got to!'

'**Look what I found.**' George held out the **box.** 'It was washed up on the shore. All it needs is a bit of a clean. Then it will make the **perfect present** for Alf.'

'That's not the **only** thing that needs
a bit of a clean!' Aunt Fanny scolded, looking
down at George's sandy feet.

'**I'm sorry**, everyone,' George said, looking round at Julian, Dick and Anne who had come to join them. 'I really shouldn't have been so **beastly** earlier.'

'Already forgotten,' said Julian.

'We got some wonderful **presents** for Alf this morning. We bought him **a book of adventure stories,'** said Anne.

'And I chose him a **whistle**,' added Dick.

'How marvellous!' said George. **'He'll love those!'**

'Now come on,' said Aunt Fanny, 'you'd

better wrap those presents. There's some wrapping paper in the drawer. Then you really must get going to the **party,** or you'll be late.'

George **hurried into the kitchen** and started to polish the little box. In no time at all it was as good as new. She wrapped it up, then hurried up the stairs to get ready.

As George ran upstairs, something **caught Timmy's attention** at the kitchen window and he **growled suspiciously.** Two faces were peering into Kirrin Cottage, eying up the neatly wrapped box on the table. It was the **two men from the beach!**

CHAPTER FOUR

'Did you **hear** what that woman said?' the taller of the two men said to the other as they peered in through the window. 'Those children are going to a party and **our box** is going to be a present.'

'**You** should have been more careful, and made sure the bag was **done up tight,**' said the other. '**Trust you** to drop **the box.**'

'Well, it's no good crying over spilt milk,' said his friend. '**Now's our chance** to snatch it back.'

The two men were just about to sneak into the kitchen when Aunt Fanny swept back through the door and picked up the present.

'Come on, children,' she called.

The men slunk back into the shadows as Julian, Dick and Anne came running down the stairs, followed by George and Timmy.

The Five set off with their gifts. It wasn't a long walk into town from Kirrin Cottage – just along the **clifftops** and down **Windy Hill** – and they chatted happily as they strolled. Soon they had passed **the dairy** where they often had **ice creams**, and were on the main road into Kirrin. They reached the **ironmonger's** and headed up

to the **town hall,** where the **party** was being held. Other children carrying gifts were making their way inside.

They climbed up the steps. **'Golly! What a party!'** Dick exclaimed after they had pushed back the door.

'Doesn't it look wonderful?' Anne agreed, as they looked around the room to where **streamers** and **banners** decorated every corner.

And at the far end of the hall was the best sight of all – a long table **simply groaning with food.** There were **sandwiches** piled high, delicious-smelling **sausage rolls,** an enormous **potato salad,** bright red

radishes in a big glass dish and a huge jug of homemade **lemonade!** For pudding, **jam tarts** glistened in neat rows and there were **traffic light jellies** in red, orange and green.

It all looked delicious. The Five didn't think they'd ever seen such **a feast!**

CHAPTER FIVE

A fresh-faced boy with tousled hair came **rushing over** to them, grinning. **'Hallo, all of you,'** he said.

It was Alf, and he was followed by a man with a weather-beaten face, white hair and eyes as **blue as the sea**. **'This is my grandfather,'** he said.

'Very pleased to meet you,' said Julian, holding out his hand. 'I'm Julian. This is my brother Dick and my sister Anne, and this is our cousin George.'

'It's lovely to meet you all. And who's this handsome fellow?'

'This is my dog, Timmy,' said George, beaming.

'Happy Birthday, Alf,' said Julian, handing him the parcel. **'Go on, open it now!'**

Alf tore off the paper and exclaimed with **delight** when he saw the book inside. Then he opened Dick's present and blew the whistle.

'And here's one from me,' said George, holding out her present. 'But you need to open it carefully as it's a little **fragile.'**

Alf slowly peeled back the paper. 'Oh, what a **beautiful box!'** **he cried,** **lifting the lid.** 'It's just the thing for storing my fishing tackle.'

Alf's grandfather was looking very closely at the **gleaming box.** 'Well, I never!' he whispered to himself. **'I can't believe it.** I've seen this box before, **long, long ago.** You've heard stories about your great-grandfather, Alf? The one you were named after?'

The boy nodded.

'He was a skilled sailor, **and this box belonged to him.** I used to help him pack his things inside it before he went on long trips at sea, but it was lost during a **terrible storm** when his ship was wrecked. I never thought I'd see it again! Wherever did you find it?'

'It was down on the beach,' said George. 'Washed up with the tide.'

'But how can you be sure it's the same box?' asked Julian.

'Look here,' the man replied. He lifted up one of the sides to reveal a **hidden compartment.** A drawer popped out, and inside was a small **golden compass.** It had glass over the front and a red arrow across the middle and there were some initials engraved on the back casing.

'The same initials as mine!' said Alf, amazed. 'What an **incredible** present. Thank you so much, George. **This is the best birthday ever.'**

George swelled with pride. She was delighted that her present had made him so happy.

'You'll have to look after it, Alf. Boxes like this are very rare and worth quite a bit of money these days,' said the boy's grandfather. **'Right.** Let's put the presents over here. Time for some **party games**, I think!'

CHAPTER SIX

The **party** was in full swing by the time the two strangers reached the town hall. They had followed the group from a safe distance and stopped on the way to dress up as **clowns** – the perfect disguise for a party!

Now they were peering through a window of the town hall. While the children played **musical chairs** and **blind man's buff,** the two men waited for their chance. The presents had been left on a table, unattended.

'**Come on, Timmy,**' Anne called. 'You can play too.'

But Timmy didn't want to join in the games. He had spotted the unwelcome visitors.

'Woof-woof! **WOOF!**' he barked at the window.

George turned as the men ducked back down. 'There's **nobody** there, Tim,' she said.

The children went back to the games while Timmy kept his eyes **fixed** on the window.

'If only that dratted dog would get out of the way,' one of the men said to the other. **'I'll distract him. You grab the box**.'

The two men slipped inside. While one of them tried to get Timmy's attention, the other hurried over to the table and **snatched the box.** Quick as a **flash,** he tore across the room to the door, while his companion also

made a break for it. But Timmy wasn't going to let them get away with the treasure.

He grabbed the trouser leg of the thief with the box, who **stumbled and fell into the other man.** They both landed in a groaning heap on the floor.

Timmy stood over the men, growling. **They were caught!**

Their **shouts** attracted the attention of the guests, who turned to see what was going on.

'**Clowns?** We weren't expecting any entertainment!' exclaimed Alf's grandfather.

As the men slowly sat up, rubbing their heads, their red noses and wigs fell off.

'**It's you . . . the men from Kirrin Bay!**' George cried, explaining to everyone how she had seen them only that morning, acting suspiciously. She spotted the box on the floor next to them. 'Look, Alf, they're trying to **steal** your **box!**'

'Well, we won't be having any of that,' said Alf's grandfather, striding over. '**What do you think you're doing?**'

'This is **our box**,' said the other man. 'We **dropped it** on the beach earlier this morning.'

'That be may so,' the older man said, '**but the rightful owner of this box was my father** – his initials are on the compass inside it.

Let's call the **police!** I'm sure they'll have something to say about this!'

CHAPTER SEVEN

The two men tried to make **a run for it,**
but they were held down by Alf's grandfather
and another adult until the **police got there.**
'Well, well, well,' said one of
the police inspectors as they walked in. 'Look

what we have here. We've been after this pair for some time now – they've been going up and down the coast, **stealing boats and equipment** from fishermen and **plundering local wrecks.'**

George told the inspectors what she had worked out for herself – **that the men had seen her pick up the box from the beach,** then followed her all the way to

Kirrin Cottage and then to the party. No wonder she had had the feeling that someone was watching her.

'Alf will be able to keep the box, though, won't he?' George said, looking worriedly from one inspector to the other as the two men were put in **handcuffs.**

'He certainly will,' said one of the police

CLICK

inspectors. 'The box belongs to the family of its original owner.'

Hoorah! The Five breathed a sigh of relief and gave a loud cheer.

'**What a thrill** you and Timmy have had today, George,' said Julian. 'Finding the box on the beach, the party and then capturing a pair

of **thieves!'**

'Indeed!' said Alf's grandfather as he came into the room carrying the **most enormous cake** they had ever seen. It was shaped like a treasure chest with chocolate coins surrounding it.

'Good job the thieves didn't manage to get their hands on the **real** treasure,' said Dick, eying up the cake. Everyone laughed.

Once Alf had blown out his candles, the cake was cut into slices and passed around. They all agreed it was **awfully good.**

'Haven't we **forgotten someone?'** asked George.

'I don't think so,' said Anne, looking around the room as everyone was **happily munching.**

George laughed. **'I mean Timmy!** Doesn't he deserve a slice of **cake** too? We wouldn't have captured the thieves without him!'

'It's true,' said Dick. 'What do you think, Timmy?' he asked as Alf's grandfather placed **a slice of cake in front of the hero of the day.**

'Woof!' said Timmy.
'Woof-woof! WOOF!'

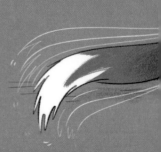

THE END

COMING SOON!

THE FAMOUS FIVE

FIVE TO THE RESCUE

A newly created **COLOUR** *Short Story*

Illustrated by **Becka Moor**

If you enjoyed this Famous Five short story, there's plenty more action and adventure in the full-length Famous Five novels. Here is a list of all the titles, in the order they were first published.